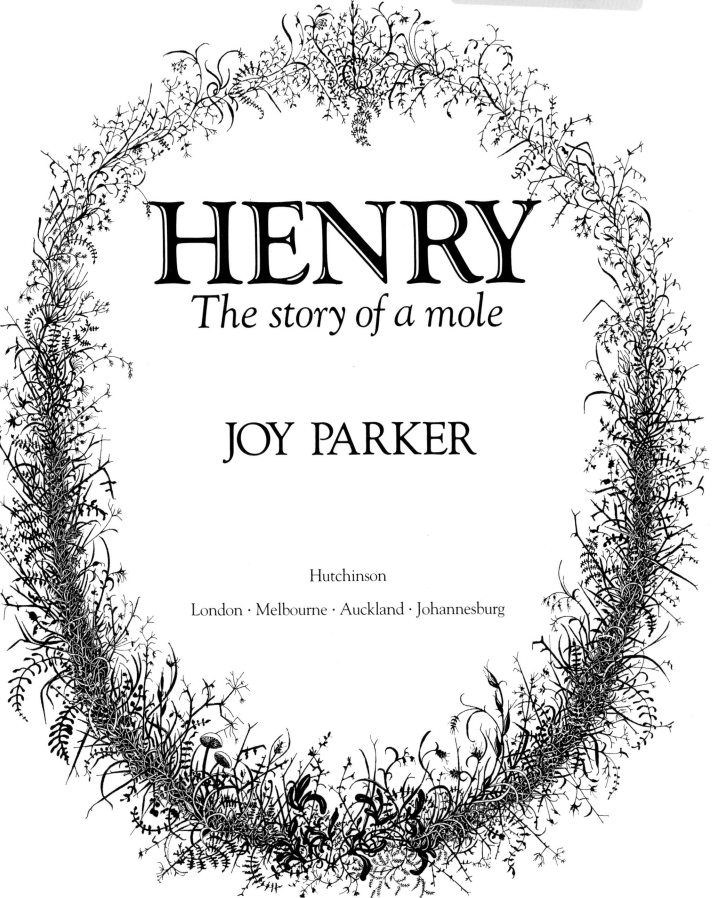

HENRY
The story of a mole

JOY PARKER

Hutchinson

London · Melbourne · Auckland · Johannesburg

This is the story of a mole.
His name was Henry.
Sometimes he was a happy mole.

Sometimes he was moody.

Sometimes he was a studious mole.

Sometimes  he was merry.

He lived in the middle of a field with many other moles, and he was a most ordinary mole – except for one thing which was extraordinary.

He was white.

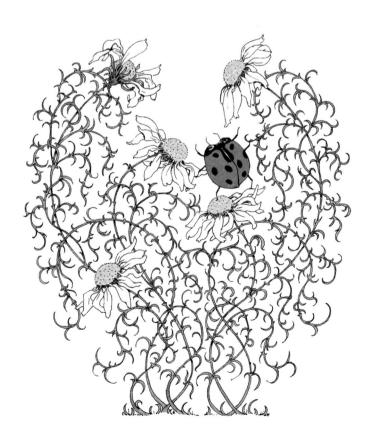

All moles are mole coloured.

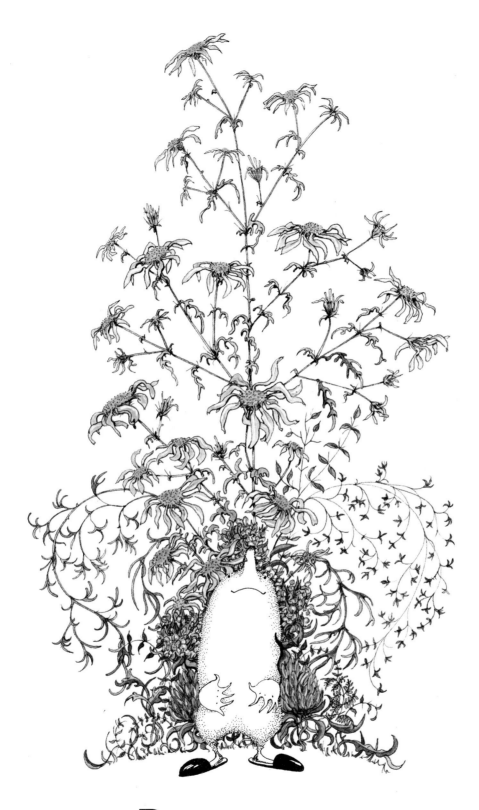

But Henry Mole was quite white.

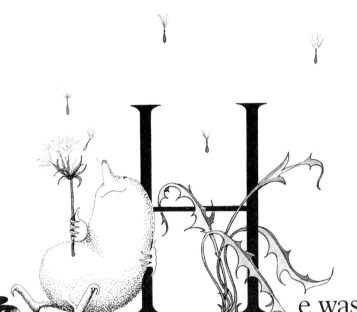 e was so proud of
his beautiful, white fur that
he could not bear to get it dirty;
he idled away the hours,
admiring his reflection

and brushing his coat.

The other moles thought him lazy, and grumbled as they tunnelled that he was growing very vain. They asked him to take part in a burrowing competition, and when he replied, 'Oh but I couldn't,' they decided that he was rather rude.

After this, no one spoke to him.

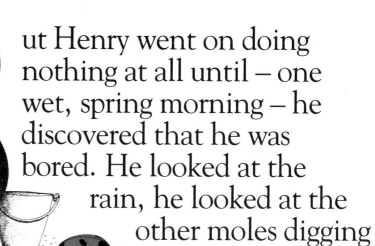

ut Henry went on doing nothing at all until – one wet, spring morning – he discovered that he was bored. He looked at the rain, he looked at the other moles digging in the sticky soil and he said to himself, 'I'm tired of that rain, I'm tired of those moles and I'm tired of the mud on my clean kitchen floor.'
He put on his boots and left.

 e walked,

and he walked,

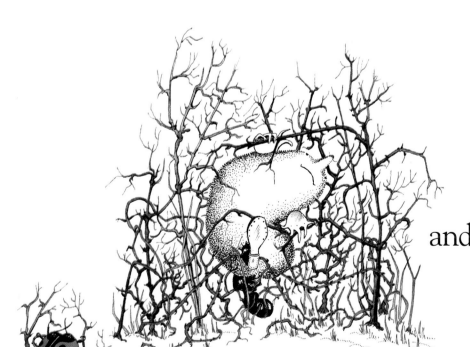

and he walked...

until he came to the sea. There he saw
a ship setting sail for the North Pole.
'A good beginning!' he cried.

SAILINGS
10 AM. ROUND THE BAY
11 AM PROSPERO'S ISLAND
12·0 TO THE NORTH POLE·

I t was a beautiful voyage.
The sea was dark green, the waves were white and crisp.
As Henry stood on the prow of the ship a breeze
ruffled his fur.

When they reached the frozen North,
'This is for me!' he shouted and leapt into
the snow. 'How white, how cool, how clean!'
he cried. 'Oh joy, oh bliss! I am a snow mole
and I shall stay here for ever!'

He dived into a deep
drift and disappeared.

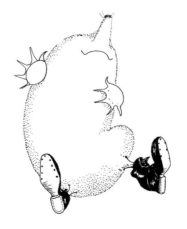

urprised by the sound of shouting and
strange laughter, the animals of the
frozen North came hurrying across the ice.
A polar bear crouched low in the snow.
'Who are you?' he asked.
'I'm Henry Mole,' said Henry and bowed.
'What is a mole?' asked Polar Bear.
Henry told him.
'They burrow and dig,' he explained,
'and are clever with their hands. Other moles are
mole coloured, but I'm different because I'm white;
I hate mud, and this snow is just what I've been
looking for.'
'Amazing,' said Polar Bear.

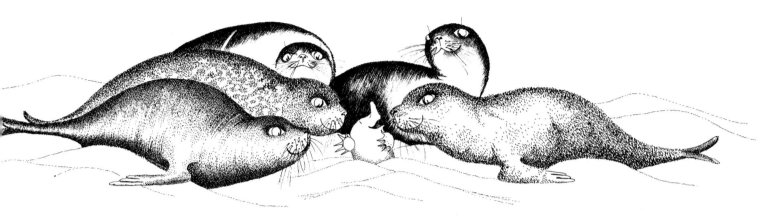

Several seals slid nearer to look.

'Do you really make snow hills with your own hands? Show us again!' they barked.

So Henry dived and burrowed in his most spectacular manner until the sun went down behind the ice mountains, and the sky turned from blue to green.

'Time to make for home,' cried Polar Bear, stamping his paws. 'Henry Mole you must be our guest. We are delighted to have you here. A fresh face – such entertainment! You are very welcome.'

'How kind of you,' said Henry and hurried his steps to keep pace with him.

They all crowded into Polar Bear's igloo.
It was very warm inside. Polar Bear lit the
lamp and opened the glowing stove. 'Food!' he cried,
tying on a large apron.

'Ah!' said Henry. 'What do you folk eat
round here?'

'Fish,' said Polar Bear. 'There's nothing
else; but oh – such variety! Such flavour!'

The seals smacked their lips and murmured,
'Fish!'

Then Polar Bear took down a large frying pan
and the igloo was filled with the sound of sizzling
and the most delicious smell.

When the last fish was eaten, everyone
said, 'Goodnight.'
    Henry sat by the stove and licked his fingers
one by one. 'What a day!' he said to himself.

Then Polar Bear turned down the lamp and
they climbed into their bunks.
    All next day Henry burrowed
and made snow hills and in the evening
they had another fish supper.
    So every day was the same and as
beautiful as the day before; and
Henry's fur was as white as the snow.

uddenly one morning the sky was clouded
and dark. Such a freezing wind whistled round
the igloo that Henry stayed huddled inside.
The next day was the same; so was the nex

Henry became depressed, he lost his appetite for fish.
'The sun can't shine every day,' said Polar Bear.
'You should see the storms in the winter months.
It's dark all the time and the lamps are lit
all day long.'
Henry was horrified.
How awful, he thought.

Then he sneezed.

'Now I've caught a cold,' he grumbled,
and he crept into his bunk and pulled the blankets
over his head.   'Oh, I am ill,' he moaned.

Polar Bear took his temperature and was cheerful and brisk. 'Not very ill,' he said, 'just a chill.' And he filled a hot-water bottle.

Henry was a bad patient and fussed about his pillows.

When he was better, he stood at the door
of the igloo listlessly looking at the snow.
He no longer wanted to burrow or dig, it made
his fur wet and his feet cold. He grew so
irritable that Polar Bear avoided him, and the
seals said, 'Henry Mole is a bore.'

He went for walks by himself, feeling
chilled and alone.

ne day while he was out,

it began to snow.

The flakes
whirled thickly
about his head, making
him dizzy and hiding his path. 'Oh I am lost!' he cried.
The blizzard stopped and it grew dark and
very still. Henry was afraid. 'Polar Bear. Where
are you?' he called. But his own voice answered
from the ice mountains.
'You – oo – oo!' it echoed in the freezing air.
He tried to run, slipping and stumbling in the
deep drifts. He skidded and went spinning
into the dark.
'Where am I now?' he wailed.

The wind blew the clouds from the moon,
and Henry saw that he was surrounded by ice.

He burst into tears.

Tears ran down his nose and
began to melt the ice around him.

With a small, scrunchy
sound it broke from the rest – and he floated
out to sea.
'Help!' he cried.

The tide carried him away from the frozen
North towards the warm waters of the South.
'My ice will melt,' Henry said to himself
but, as it disappeared beneath his boots, he
saw a sail.

'Saved!' he cried,
and sank into the sea.

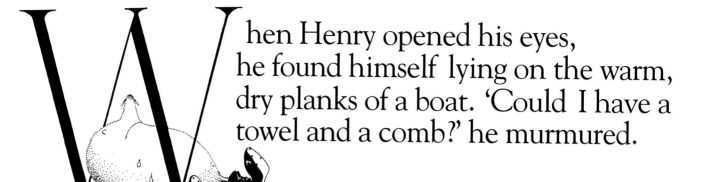

When Henry opened his eyes, he found himself lying on the warm, dry planks of a boat. 'Could I have a towel and a comb?' he murmured.

But instead of soothing sounds of sympathy he heard harsh voices shouting, 'Look 'ere!' and 'What's this?' Two fierce fishermen tied him up with string and tossed him among the hooks and harpoons.

'Take it back alive,' growled one.

'Use it for bait,' snarled the other.

They began to quarrel, then they began to fight. A knife flashed. Everything rocked.

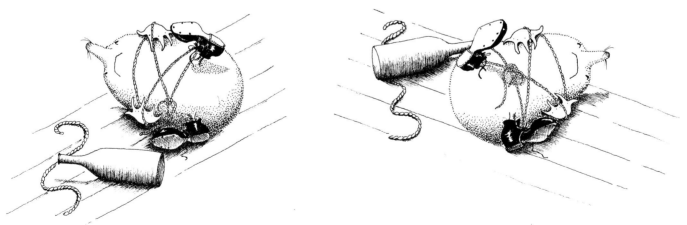

With a shout and a splash the fishermen disappeared... the boat floated on....

'Adrift and alone,' moaned Henry, struggling with the string.

'Can I help you?' said a soft voice in his ear. 'My name is Daphne.' Standing by his side was a beautiful seagull.

'I'm Henry Mole,' said Henry. 'Get me out of this string.'

Daphne pecked with her beak until it broke. 'Free!' she murmured, and Henry laughed and stretched and stamped his feet.

'Now! Can you fly?' she asked.

'Moles don't fly,' said Henry.

'Then we must stay here,' said Daphne, 'and see which way the current carries us!'

They settled themselves among the nets
and Henry suddenly felt very happy drifting
along in the sunshine with Daphne for company.
'How pleasant this is,' he murmured. 'I
should have been a sailor mole – sailing the
high seas.'
'I smell rain,' said Daphne.

'Come rain, come wind,'
Henry cried, 'this is the life for me!'

In the distance thunder rumbled and a
sudden wind rippled the water. Big drops of
rain began to fall. Henry shivered and hid
beneath Daphne's wing.

ll night they tossed in a terrible storm. When morning came, Daphne saw that they were drifting towards jagged rocks. 'Henry,' she cried, 'I must save you!' Henry looked at the choppy water; he felt very ill.

'Leave me here to die,' he groaned.

'Don't be silly,' said Daphne. 'Climb on my back; take hold of the feathers at my neck.'

'But I've never flown,' wept Henry.

'Hurry!' shrieked Daphne.

Henry shut his eyes and clung to her. The boat struck the rocks—

As the wood splintered and smashed they
soared into the air.

Daphne could see land ahead. She flew on
bravely, but Henry and his boots were heavy and
the beat of her wings grew slower; she began to
lose height, but as she touched the water a
wave swept them safely on to a beach.

Daphne lay on her side, exhausted, while Henry took off his soggy boots. The sand was warm between his toes.

'Sand,' he murmured, 'clean, golden sand. It doesn't make me dirty and it doesn't make me wet.' He began to dig. 'I am a sand mole and I shall stay here for ever!' he shouted – and disappeared.

The sun went down.

Daphne preened her feathers and waited by his boots; then she sighed, slowly circled the shore and flew away.

When Henry came to the surface he felt quite tired. I wonder what happened to Daphne, he thought, and he lay down and went to sleep.

The waves lapped at his boots and carried them out to sea.

W hen Henry woke, the sun was burning in the sky.

He climbed up the beach to explore.
Here the grass was yellow and scorched; the
earth, dusty and dry.
   'This is a hot place,' he said. 'I wish
I had put on my boots.'

He met a lizard poised in his path.
'Who are you?' he asked. But the lizard
looked at him sharply and darted away.

He sat down to rest on a rock.
But the rock was a snake
which uncurled beneath him

and slid hissing into the prickly grass.
'How unfriendly everyone is,' he said.

There was no shade anywhere. On the
beach the sand burnt his toes and got into his fur.

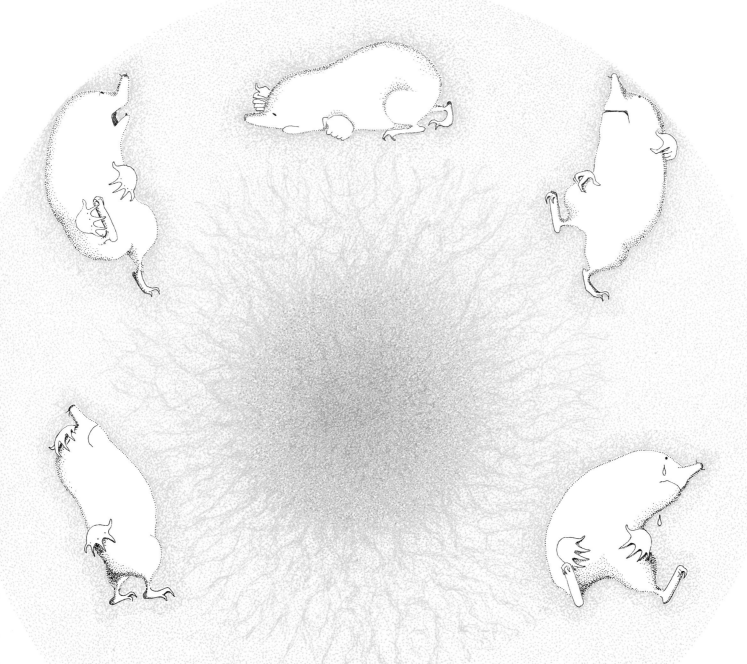

'I'm very hot and very uncomfortable,' he grumbled.
All day he lay on the beach, listless and limp.

As the sun went down he fell asleep.
When he woke the tide was coming in and Daphne
was standing by his side. 'Henry!' she cried,
'whatever is the matter?'

'Oh Daphne,' he wept, 'I think I've been a
foolish mole – rushing all over the world.
The snow was so cold and the fish tasted
horrible; now I'm too hot and there's nothing
to eat at all. I left such a green and muddy
field at home, such a cool, comfortable
burrow – the earth smelt so sweet in the rain
– all because I was proud of my beautiful
white fur.'

'Beautiful white fur!' exclaimed Daphne.
'You look black to me. It must be all this
sunbathing you've been doing.'

Henry looked at his fur, 'That's not black
– that's mole coloured,' he shouted.

'I've gone mole coloured – all over!'

They sat together by the edge of the water, and Henry admired his fur until it was too dark for him to see.

'I want to go home,' he said. 'How shall I find a way?' He nodded and dozed, but Daphne did not sleep; she watched the moon come up, she listened to the waves and heard the dolphins playing far out at sea.

'You shall go home,' she whispered. 'I have an idea!'

The sun rose on an empty beach. While Henry rode the waves on a dolphin's back, Daphne flew overhead.

hen the sun was high they saw a ship.
'For home!' shouted Henry, and
Daphne flew with him to the deck.

'Goodbye,' she said, 'you will be happy to
get home.'
'Yes I shall,' said Henry.
The dolphin laughed and
sighed and slipped away,
but Daphne drooped
her head. Then,
with a sweep of her wings,
she sailed into the sky.

Henry slept for most of the journey. When he woke, the ship was sailing into the bay. It was a beautiful morning. The sea was smooth, the land was soft and green in the early sun.

He leapt ashore and hurried home...

. . . through the summer grass.

The other moles did not recognize him
at first, but when they realized who it was
they gave him a great welcome, shaking his hand
and congratulating him on the colour of his fur.

Henry never boasted about his travels.
'I'm very happy to be home,' he said.